PLAYING WITH FYRE

FYRE & ASHES BOOK ONE

LOGAN FOX

CONTENTS

AUTHOR NOTE

This book contains mature content and content some may find triggering, including: Non-con, Dub-Con, Torture (Not FMC), Stalking, Violence (gore, murder, torture), Breath play, Bondage, Somnophilia, Kidnapping/Captivity, SA/abuse (Not on page), Suicide ideation, Drugs & alcohol. For a full list of triggers for this series, please visit the trigger page of my website at: https://authorloganfox. com/triggers

JOIN THE FOX DEN

Can I send you my secret dark romance novella that's never been published…?
Join my VIP newsletter and you'll receive your own exclusive copy of My Darling, and I'll keep you up to date with my new releases and promos!
https://authorloganfox.com/my-darling-signup

PLAYING WITH FYRE PLAYLIST

Good For You — Selena Gomez, A$AP Rocky
#1 Crush — Garbage
You're The One That I Want — Lo-Fang
I Want You to Want Me — Children of Paradise, Chantel Claret
Play with Fire — Sam Tinnesz, Yacht Money
Animals — Maroon 5
Somebody's Watching Me — Hidden Citizens
What Do I Say — Landon Tewers, Seanzy
This Empty Love — Innerpartysystem
Happy Together — Spin
Monster Inside — Ilya ID & I, The Ocean

1

CHARLOTTE

My gaze is glued to Professor Gideon Fyre's tall, commanding frame as he stalks through the clinically neat arrangement of tables, easels, and workbenches inside his classroom. Every few seconds he'll stop beside someone, whether they're standing or sitting, and murmur a few words to them. I can't help but watch him, and it's not just because he's handsome. He has power over me—over everyone—and it's obvious he knows it.

Today's art therapy class is about identifying. Identifying with ourselves, identifying the root of our issues. We're eight weeks into our course at the local community college. I never thought art could be so...well, therapeutic, but the credit undoubtedly goes to Professor Fyre.

When I laid eyes on him the first time, I thought I'd walked into the wrong classroom. Tall and broad-shouldered with thick dark hair, he didn't look like a college professor. He introduced himself with a laundry list of qualifications during that first lesson—including but not limited to a psychology *and* an art degree. He also told us he enjoys heading out to his cabin in the mountains for some deer hunting when his schedule allows.

Professor Fyre looks up. Our eyes lock, and I blush crimson. When he heads in my direction, I quickly go back to my scribbling. He encourages us to use any medium we want. Something that speaks to us. That expresses our emotions. That ruled out pasta art—I went straight for a thick piece of charcoal and got my fingers dirty.

Now they're pitch black, just like my soul.

"That's the first time I've seen you smile, Charlotte," a voice murmurs beside my ear.

I drop my piece of charcoal. Fyre knows he's dealing with goddamn trauma victims—how dare he sneak up on his students?

"I smile all the time."

"Less often than you lie, it seems."

I stiffen. "You said we're supposed to concentrate. Can't go around grinning like an idiot."

He's standing so close I can smell his cologne—earthy, woody, and spicy, just like I imagine his cabin must smell like—and feel the warmth of his body, despite the layers of clothing I'm bundled up in because the heating is on the fritz. Pneumonia wouldn't be the worst thing that's happened to me the past few months.

Fuck…it wouldn't even crack the top five.

Fyre lets out a low chuckle that makes my insides tingle in response. How often does he go to his hunting cabin? Has he ever considered taking one of his students with him?

Ha! A man like him? He says he does this class because he loves helping people discover themselves, but I've seen how the other college students and teachers treat him out in the hall. He has clout. Probably getting tenure in a few years. He's at least a decade older than me, and that should put my fantasies to rest, but it just makes me wonder what it's like to be with an older man. Especially one as mindbogglingly good-looking as him. With his dark hair, and his warm brown eyes. Those thick brows and strong nose. The dimple in his chin and the sensuous curve of his mouth.

Fyre makes a sound in the back of his throat. Does he know what I'm thinking? My heart pounds at the thought.

"Are you challenging yourself, Charlotte?"

I quiver at the sound of my name. It happens whenever he speaks to me.

Professor Fyre crouches beside my chair, laying a hand on the desk before grabbing the back of my chair with the other. He brushes my shoulder, and that touch sends a shiver through me that I barely suppress.

I stare at the sheet of paper in front of me. I never know what I'm going to draw—I just pick up a piece of charcoal and start doodling. He told us this wasn't an art class, so what is he expecting from me?

"I want you to bleed," he says.

I turn to stare at him, my lips parting. His dark eyes have the tiniest flecks of gold in them. Heat flashes onto my cheeks when I realize he's studying me as openly as I'm studying him. Which doesn't explain why he looks so fascinated. I'm as interesting as a brick.

"Bleed?" I murmur.

"Slice yourself open, Charlotte. Pour all your anger, your rage, your *pain*—" he glances away, taps the corner of my black drawing "—onto this page."

It's difficult, but I finally manage to face forward again. "But…I have."

He grasps my wrist, but as soon as we make contact he tugs his hand away like I burned him. His fleeting touch leaves behind an ephemeral ache. "Dig deeper, Charlotte. Dig until you see bone."

I'm still trying to catch my breath when his warmth fades away. My head is forward, my chin dipped down. I scan the class through my curtain of black hair. Fyre reappears a few tables away. He walks with his hands tucked behind his back, gripping his wrists, his eyes darting to every artwork he passes.

I can still hear his voice.

I can still feel his touch.

He glances across the room as if he knows I'm watching and gives me a faint, knowing smile.

Look away, Charlotte!

But I can't. I'm transfixed. This must be what a deer feels like when he's scoping them with his rifle.

"Sometimes it's difficult to expose your most hidden self when there are strangers around," Fyre says, his eyes on me. I'm convinced he's talking just to me, but then his gaze flicks to someone else.

I let out a soft, rueful laugh and drop my head. Why on earth do I have this recurring fantasy that the world revolves around me? I'm one of his students. A troubled soul in need of healing. That's it.

"Well done, everyone. You can put away your things." There's a general clatter and shuffling as my classmates start packing up. Fyre watches them, and I watch Fyre. As soon as everyone's settled back in their seats, he says, "I have another assignment for the class."

My fingers become jittery. I like Fyre's assignments—he always gives us interesting ways to apply our creativity. Even me with my lowly piece of charcoal. Last week's lesson was hope.

"You will begin a new project."

I purse my lips and glance around at some of the other students. It's weird calling them that since they range in ages anywhere from fifteen to seventy. But we have something in common. We've all been attacked and left traumatized.

By disease. By a criminal. By an event or significant other in our lives.

Some of the students shared their stories during that first class. I wasn't one of them. I don't think I'll ever be able to share what happened with another human being. It was traumatic enough when I had to give my statement at the police station, then again when I was assigned a therapist. Even *she* doesn't know everything, despite prying session after session after goddamn session. I have to see her again later this month, and I'm already dreading it.

"This time, you'll work in the privacy of your own home, or any other place where you feel safe." The professor's voice draws my attention back to him. Not that it's ever off him for long. "Your project must be completed by the end of this semester."

A few heads turn to look at each other. Winter break is a month away. Four more lessons, then my art therapy classes are over.

Forever.

"And you will use a different medium than the one you've been using in class."

I look down at my mess of charcoal scratchings. What? This is all I know. What the hell does he want from me, a finger painting?

"And class, I need this piece to tell a story. *Your* story."

It feels like I've just swallowed ten frozen lead weights. My first instinct is to throw up my hands and storm out of class.

Who gave him the right to snoop? I came here because my counselor suggested it. Because I was so doped up on anti-depressants she had to prescribe me shit for the side effects. She told me this class was a safe space, that I'd never have to talk about what happened if I didn't want to.

Telling *my story* doesn't sound like me not having to talk about what happened.

Somehow I swallow down the rage and the sullen, angry ache in my lower belly that never goes away. The doctor told me I'd healed down there, that I shouldn't be experiencing any pain, and refused to prescribe me more Oxy. He probably thought I was addicted after all the morphine I had in the hospital. But I'm not imagining it.

I breathe, I hurt.

I'm already craving that small pill in my nightstand, the one that sends me into oblivion, the one that stops everything. The anger, the pain…the *memories*. Something to help me sleep, but it does more than that. It frees me.

The bell sounds for the end of class. The other students begin to file out, but I'm still wrangling with my emotions. I manage to calm myself by the time the last person—an elderly woman with a headscarf that makes me think she's fighting something terminal—walks out of the door.

Fyre looks up, and there's not a trace of surprise on his face when he sees I'm still in my seat.

"I'm counting on you," he says, remaining standing behind his desk as if it's a trench between two warring nations. "Don't let me down, Charlotte."

I was going to tell him I won't do it. That it wasn't part of the deal. But then he smiles at me, and that smile promises so many things. So I nod. Dip my head. Gather up my things and shove them in my bag as I hurry for the door.

"Remember, I'm always here to help."

I stall by the door, look back at him. "What?"

His smile is still there. It feels even warmer now. Even more genuine. But I guess that's just the teacher in him. The healer.

He walks up to me and holds out a slip of paper. There's a telephone number on it. I know I shouldn't take it. It's all kinds of wrong. But I can't stop myself. Our fingers touch, electric.

He doesn't let go. "Call me anytime. Day or night."

"Why-why would I need to call you?" I ask weakly as I struggle with the myriad butterflies suddenly swarming in my stomach.

"Because I'll always be there for you." His chest expands as he inhales, and his eyes touch my mouth. "Anytime. Anywhere."

I tug the paper out of his grip and scurry out of his class like I'm being dragged by wild horses.

Hope. It's something I hadn't felt in months until last week's assignment. My piece for that theme was a glossy-black charcoal mess, of course. But the half-hour I spent on it was one of the few times I didn't think about killing myself.

2

FYRE

Charlotte is special. I've been holding these art therapy classes for three years, and I've never met a student like her. Her uniqueness would explain why I've been following her home every day since she joined my class, why I watch her as she draws in my classroom.

I'm hoping that's why I'm considering pulling over my truck and finally giving her a ride home. I've been flirting with the idea for weeks, but I've been holding back because I know it will change everything between us.

I'm not sure she's ready for the next step yet.

Charlotte is on her bike a few yards ahead of me, plowing through rain puddles with grim determination, her black hair in ribbons down the side of her face. She makes no attempt to shield herself from the rain. It's like she doesn't even realize she's soaked through.

It's easy to imagine how that wet fabric will cling to her skin when she undresses at home—as reluctant to leave her body as I am to stop watching her.

I won't lie. It's become an obsession.

And it's getting worse.

I've never given my students homework. Not once. But I saw

attraction in Charlotte's eyes today. She's trying to fight her feelings, hell so am I, but she'll lose the fight.

I have.

Ahead, the light at the intersection changes to amber. The universe, it seems, is tossing me a bone. I speed up before detouring to the side of the road, slowing hurriedly so I won't spray Charlotte with the rainwater puddling by the sidewalk. I honk the horn, but she doesn't look back. She would have been gone a second later had a car not skipped the intersection ahead and turned right in front of her, speeding so it won't have to stop at a red light.

My heart flies to my throat, and I'm only dimly aware of rain hitting my face as I kick open the truck's door.

"Charlotte!"

Her wet hair swings in the air as she whips her head around to stare at me. My loafers splat wetly on the sidewalk as I slow from a sprint to a jog. She gives me a double take and then shakes her head. "Professor Fyre?"

God, I love the sound of my name on her tongue. "Are you alright?"

Her lips part, and my cock hardens—just like it does in class when her mouth forms that same shape. I've had to come up with ingenious ways to hide my erection whenever Charlotte's in my classroom. It's laughable how many times it's happened.

I'm aware that I should explain why I'm here, but instead I say, "That idiot could have hit you."

"But he didn't." Her frown deepens. "What are you doing here?"

Swiping wet hair out of my face, I give her a lopsided smile. "I wasn't following you, if that's what you're thinking," I tell her through a laugh.

Her lips seal into a tight little smile. She balances easily on the bike for such a slip of a girl, and from how her body moves, she looks like she wants to start pedaling again.

She scrunches up her nose. "Then what are you doing here?"

The lie comes easy. "Meeting a patient at her office. She's a few blocks down from here." I point at one of the tall office buildings littering this street. This isn't the greatest neighborhood, but I'm aware that most of my students usually can't afford better accommodation.

"I didn't know you still practice," she says.

I don't. Not after Red Friday when my entire world fell apart—and I became unhinged. I could no longer stand those intimate face-to-face meetings. Depression, anger management, grief, they would just keep pouring burning oil over my soul. I left my practice, my home, the tattered remains of my life behind and started fresh here at the college.

But my Charlotte doesn't have to know that. There are many things she doesn't have to know, and I prefer to keep it that way.

For her safety, and my sanity.

"Please—" I half-turn and gesture at my truck. "Let me take you where you need to be. I can't stand the thought of you riding around in this weather. Not with these idiots on the road."

Her lips twitch, and her eyebrows draw together. She balances on the bike again, a second away from pedaling off. "What about your meeting?"

Rain starts trickling down the back of my jacket. "I'll call ahead, tell her I'll be late." I flick my head, sending rain-slicked hair off my forehead.

"Really, I'm fine."

Christ. If I had fucking candy, I'd be using that to lure her into my truck. But I can't push this. She has to make the decision herself.

"Okay. But I won't accept any excuses for that project being late, even pneumonia." I smile easily at her, turn, and head back to my truck. I shove a hand in the pocket of my trench coat and use it to keep my dick flattened. Just the thought that she might have accepted my invitation is giving me a hard-on.

The rain is insistent enough, cold enough, wet enough that Charlotte makes up her mind a few seconds later.

"Professor!"

I give my dick a relentless squeeze, willing it to subside, and glance at her over my shoulder. She's biting down on her bottom lip as she takes a quick scan around, and then hurries up to me.

I can already feel her skin against mine. Wet from the rain, wet from something else entirely.

"Good girl," I murmur as I reach for her bike's handlebars.

She freezes, blinks, and dismisses what she thinks she heard as a blush creeps onto her cheeks. I love that shy look. Her hair's too wet now, but when it's dry and she ducks her chin like that, a black curtain falls in front of her face. Every time she does it, I have to stop myself from going over and smoothing those raven locks away from her face. It would raise too many questions, and if there's one thing I've learned, it's how to avoid questions.

I take her bike and wheel it to my truck, easily imitating a sane, helpful college professor. It should come easily enough—I've been playing the part for years now. By the time I've secured her bike in the back of my truck and slid into the driver's seat, I'm just as wet as Charlotte. She throws me another shy glance from the passenger seat as I twist to the side to put on my seatbelt.

"Thanks," she murmurs, and then scoops wet hair from her face and twists it into a knot at the base of her neck.

"How could I ignore a lady in distress?"

She lets out a huff and rolls her eyes at *lady*, but the corner of her mouth curls up. We sit for a second, rain drumming on the roof of my car. I'd have let the moment go on for eternity if it meant I could keep breathing the same air as her, but it's too soon. I have to keep up appearances.

I'm her teacher, not her lover.

Not yet, anyway.

I clear my throat. "So, I could try and guess where you live, but then you might not get home in time for supper. What would your boyfriend say?"

She jumps a little and then laughs. "God, sorry." She points. "Make a left two blocks down."

"Sure thing." I make sure my voice is cheery even though I'm far from happy. This shitty neighborhood gets worse the further west you go, and if she's going where I think she's going...

"So, uh, have you seen me before?" Her voice is soft, almost meek. For a second, I wonder if that's how she always was, or if this is the new her. I've had firsthand experience in how trauma can change a person.

"Yes, of course. You were in my class an hour ago."

She laughs again, louder this time. "No, I mean—" She cuts off. "When you're meeting your patient."

"Of course I have. It's impossible to miss your black hair."

She blushes at this and bunches her hands in her lap. We're barely more than two feet apart, but that just reminds me how much closer we were earlier today.

Christ, I shouldn't have done it. Shouldn't have entered her personal space like that. Anyone could have noticed. If they'd reported it to the Dean, she'd have asked questions. There are many things I shouldn't have done. But I'm not perfect. No one is. Everyone makes mistakes. Like the one I'm planning to make with Charlotte.

It could cost me everything. My position at the college, my career...my life. I've been trying to talk myself out of it for weeks already, with no success. I want to see those small, pale hands trembling. I want them running down my belly and wrapping around my cock. I want to stare into Charlotte's sea-green eyes as she opens that pretty little mouth of hers so I can shove my cock down her throat.

I want it so bad, I dream about it.

"Right up ahead."

I blink, my mind scurrying to recall the last few minutes of the real world as I hastily shove away the image of young Charlotte moaning around my thick cock.

"This isn't the best area," I say grimly. "You bike home all the time?"

"It's not so bad."

I suppress a growl at her casual response. With both windows closed, her smell is intense, intoxicating. My blood is singing in my veins, and it takes every molecule of discipline I have not to pull the car over and shove my hand between her legs. And then take her to her apartment, pack her things, and move her into a better apartment. One where she'll be safe. One where she'll be close.

Fighting off those thoughts, I duck my head and scan the apartment blocks ahead. "Which one, Charlotte?"

When I glance at her, her face looks carved from white marble. Then she blinks, her lips parting and tongue darting out to wet them.

Jesus Christ, if she knew how close I was to turning this truck around and just—

"That one," she says, pointing past my shoulder.

She must have seen something in my eyes, heard a tremor in my voice, because the truck barely stops before she's outside, struggling to get her bike off the back of the truckbed. I watch her in the rearview mirror for a few seconds, composing myself, before stepping out to help her. But by the time I get to the back, her bike is on the ground and she's swiping damp hair from her face with the back of her hand.

"Thank you," she blurts out, and then hurries down the road.

She's going in the wrong direction. We passed her apartment half a block ago.

Clever little girl, leading the wolf astray. She doesn't seem to realize that I'll always be able to find her, now that I have her scent.

3

CHARLOTTE

The Sizzling Griddle diner is always packed on a Friday night, but it's the closest decent restaurant to my apartment. Here, I can order a cheeseburger and fries and not feel like I'm consuming half a gallon of cooking oil on the side.

But they're so busy that the only option when the craving hits me on the weekend is walking two blocks to go fetch my order, or wait an hour for my food.

I'm not a patient woman.

Which is why I'm glaring at the back of a guy's head, the one who's been standing at the front of the queue for ten minutes because he can't make up his mind about what he wants to order. I'm about to go over there and demand he falls back in line until he's ready when an invisible touch strokes the skin between my shoulder blades.

Through a brief lull in the ambient chatter-clatter of the diner, I hear the jangle of the door's bell. I turn, glance at the man who's stepped inside, and face forward again. Then I do a double take.

It's Professor Fyre.

Suddenly, my lust for a juicy cheeseburger is snuffed out. Something else replaces it…something much, much more carnal.

I'm starting to sweat.

It has nothing to do with the temperature inside the diner, or the jacket I threw on when I left my apartment, or even the walk over here.

It's all him.

I can feel him behind me.

I'm still mind-blown about the fact that he gave me a ride home earlier this week. I know I shouldn't have said yes, but I couldn't resist him. I mean, he's handsome in class, but seeing him on the side of the street, out in the real world, was something else. Those five minutes I spent in the cab of his truck with him was the fuel for several dirty dreams and three exquisite masturbation sessions—two in the shower, one in my bed.

I just couldn't get over how fucking sexy he looked with his dark, wet hair and his concerned expression.

Wait. Why is he here? Is he…is he following me?

The hair on my arms stands up. A rush of heat floods through me, warming my already pink cheeks. I unzip my jacket and flap the two halves to try and cool down a little, but as circumspectly as I can so I don't draw Fyre's attention.

Unless he's already seen me. Shit, what if he thinks I'm avoiding him?

Now my cheeks are on fire. And the worst part is, even if I wanted to escape this infernal torture, I'd have to walk right past him to get to the door.

I'm trapped.

A trickle of sweat tickles down my back.

Think, Charlotte, think!

I jerk when my phone rings impossibly loud. Instantly, I hear a bunch of grumbles around me. I fumble in my pocket, trying desperately to silence my phone. But when I try and take it out of my pocket, it hooks on my jacket and goes flying out of my hand. I scamper after it, but a loafer comes down just right and stops it from slamming into the wall a few feet away.

My heart stutters. I recognize that shoe.

When I look up, Fyre's bronze eyes are hooded, his jaw taut. "I thought I recognized you," he murmurs, his deep voice turning into a low rumble.

He bends down and picks up my phone, dusting it off against his dark trench coat before handing it over to me. When I try and take it, he catches me in a steely grip, crushing the phone between our fingers.

I open my mouth to tell him to let go, but then he drags me closer. My eyes fly back to his, and I swallow hard, my phone forgotten in my hand.

Is he going to kiss me? He must be. Why else would he be drawing me close, scanning my face—

Someone bumps my shoulder as they squeeze past the queue.

That's why.

Because I'm in the goddamn way.

"Sorry," he says in that deep but quiet voice of his, but it's a lie. He's not sorry. Someone else pushes past me, and they're not as polite as the one before. They jar me so hard, I fall against Fyre.

His dark brows twitch. "Are you okay?"

Fuck no. I'm all hot and bothered because just last night, I fell asleep seconds after climaxing to the thought of him eating me out.

Wetness pools in my underwear.

I gasp, utter mortification staining my cheeks. I'm wearing a denim skirt and knee-high boots today, so all that's standing between me and the whole world knowing how wet this man makes me is a tiny slip of fabric—which is already soaking wet.

Twisting out of his grip, I charge out of the diner's entrance, not caring who I knock into on the way out. He calls my name, but I don't turn back.

4

CHARLOTTE

When I go to open my door almost an hour later, it's with the full expectation that it's my cat-hoarding neighbor who'll be standing there, asking me if I've seen one of her many feral cats.

But, instead, when I wrench open the door, it's Professor Fyre looming over me, not Mrs. Crawford with a cat on her arm.

Am I hallucinating? Is this some weird sex day-dream?

But no. As soon as Fyre clears his throat and holds up my phone, I know it's real because the screen is cracked.

My dreams are never this detailed.

I take my phone with trembling fingers. "Wh—How—Where—?"

"Third time lucky," he says with a half-shrug. "Is there a reason why you lied about which apartment block you live in?"

I manage a mute shake of my head. His eyes flicker past me, as if he's waiting for me to invite him inside. Instead, I push out another, "But how did you know which room—"

"You're the only Ash on the intercom system," he says.

When my shocked expression doesn't change, he adds, "I'm your therapist. I do happen to know your surname."

"B-But the buzzer didn't…" I trail off because I don't know why I keep trying to challenge the logic of this situation.

"A very kind lady let me in, but only after she made sure I didn't know anything about her missing cat."

"Mrs. Crawford let you in?" My head's swimming and I have a feeling it's to do with Fyre's frank, unblinking stare.

"You left in quite a rush," he says, mildly admonishing me with his gorgeous eyes. Then he holds up a brown paper bag printed with the name of the diner we were both just at. "Cheeseburger okay?"

I don't know how I feel about Professor Fyre sitting on my couch. Hell, I don't even know how I feel about eating in front of him. Especially since I'm starving, and goddamnit this cheeseburger is so fucking delicious. I try to restrain myself, but then I lose concentration after a bite or two and realize I'm devouring my food like my last meal was a pretzel I ate seven weeks ago.

"Damn, she wasn't kidding—they do make good burgers," Fyre says.

I've been avoiding looking in his direction as much as possible, but this has me intrigued. "She?" I ask through a mouthful of burger patty and cheese.

"Sally, my patient." Fyre stares at the window opposite us as he pops a fry into his mouth, and then glances over at me. "My session with her ran late tonight, and she recommended this place to me when I left. Guess she heard my stomach grumbling." His laugh is the warmest, richest sound I've ever heard.

How does he do it? How can this man add such vivacity to my dark, colorless world with just one laugh?

"Their burgers kick ass," I agree with a nod, "but they make a mean pizza too."

He smiles around another fry, and then his expression turns serious. "I'm concerned about you, Charlotte."

My food gets stuck in my throat. I swallow hard, but it doesn't budge. Snatching up my soda, I suck down a sweet sip. "What? Why?"

"You're acting irrationally." He glances at my cracked phone where I left it on the coffee table.

Because I ran out so fast, I left him holding my phone. Now what the hell am I supposed to say? Oh, it's nothing, Professor Fyre. I'm just hopelessly in love with you, is all. Nothing but a silly crush, I'm sure, but it makes me do stupid, stupid things.

"I got claustrophobic," I lie, not making eye contact. "I had to get out, and then I thought I was going to be sick, so I ran home."

Worst. Excuse. Ever.

"Shit," Fyre says, cocking his head to the side. "This claustrophobia, is it new?"

My stomach plunges to my feet. I look away, my hands tightening around the soda can. "No. I mean, I've had it for a few months."

That's not a lie. I do get claustrophobic when I'm in confined spaces, but not when I'm surrounded by people. I actually kind of feel safe when there are other people around. Which is weird, because I'm always looking forward to being alone.

My head is a messed up place lately.

"Claustrophobia can be treated with exposure therapy," Fyre says, his intelligent eyes locking onto me. I'm swept up, incapable of looking away as he puts down his container and shifts forward on his seat. "Is it something you'd be open to?"

"What is it?"

He smiles faintly. "Exactly what the name suggests. Your therapist would expose you to various levels of confinement—in a safe space, of course—which would gradually help you overcome the source of your anxiety."

I shake my head, just the thought making my throat close up.

Fyre chuckles. "I agree. It's not for everyone. But sometimes, exposure therapy is the only way to tackle a debilitating anxiety." He glances around my apartment. "Could you point me in the direction of your bathroom?"

Oh fuck.

"You…uh…now?" My heart starts galloping. I'm pretty sure it's a fucking mess in there. Underwear, dirty clothes. When last did I wash out the sink?

Shit, shit, shit!

"I just want to wash my hands," he says, a crooked smile jumping onto his lips.

"Oh, I just use the kitchen sink. Water pressure is much better." I stab a finger toward the basin. Not so much showing him where it is as demanding that he use it instead.

"That's terrible," he says through a laugh as he goes over to wash his hands. "Pressure that bad in the shower too?"

"Oh no, that's fine. Maybe it's from a different pipe or something." Oh my God, the lies! How am I ever going to keep all this shit straight?

Fyre wipes his hands on a paper towel he tore off from the roll tossed haphazardly onto the counter, walking closer with a broad smile on his face.

It's unreal how he fills my apartment. In the classroom, I never realized just how big he was. How tall, how broad-shouldered. But here? I feel like I've let a giant into my home.

He's headed straight for me, which I guess is the closest route back to his seat after visiting the kitchen sink. But he stops a foot away, towering over me until I'm forced to crane back my head and look up.

At the sight of his expression, I shoot to my feet.

His eyes are narrowed, his jaw bunched. "Wait a second," he says.

Oh fuck.

I want to step back, to keep away from him in case he lashes out at me. I don't know why that's suddenly a possibility, but the instant I think about it, I can't get it out of my head.

"What?"

"Your file didn't mention anything about claustrophobia."

My heart hammers in my chest.

Fyre steps closer. His full mouth is set in a straight line. "Why are you lying to me, Charlotte?"

His earthy, woody scent envelops me. I'm sucked into his eyes like they're whirlpools out on some midnight ocean.

Trapped.

My heart pounding in my chest.

But is it fear…or excitement?

He opens his mouth again, his expression becoming even sterner, and I do the only thing I can think of to stop him from interrogating me.

I kiss him.

I have to grab hold of his jacket and haul myself onto the tips of my toes to get it right, but I do it. I kiss Professor Fyre like my life depends on it. When Fyre wraps his arms around me and pulls me even closer, I can barely hold onto reality.

I've been dreaming about this moment for *weeks,* and it's just how I imagined it.

Wild, and violent, and utterly intoxicating.

5

FYRE

I'm thankful the rain has passed. Forecasts predict clear, chilly weather.

All the better to stalk you in, my dear Charlotte.

I'm parked in my Audi directly opposite her apartment building. I never drive this car to the college, so she can't know it's mine. And, with its tinted windows, she can't know that I'm inside, watching.

I'm conflicted as fuck right now. Guess I have been since the moment she laid that pretty mouth of hers on mine. Hell, maybe even before that. I was fucked the moment she first slipped silently into my class, shoulders hunched and face hidden behind her hair as if she would be all too happy if no one ever noticed her.

But I did, Charlotte. I noticed you, and I locked onto your scent, your presence, like the wolf that I am.

Now I sit here, stewing. I want to race up those stairs and demand you close your curtains so everyone and their dog can't look right into your bedroom. But *I* want to look into your bedroom, so you can't very well be closing your curtains, can you?

I rub my palms against my thighs, the thick jeans creating friction with my skin. It's ten o'clock on a Saturday night, Charlotte. Someone your age should be out dancing. Drinking with friends. Fuck it, watching a movie if you're into that. But here you are, alone in your apartment, with only your bedroom light on. At this angle, I can see a vague suggestion of a lamp and a bedpost. You haven't come close enough to the window for me to see *you*.

I jerk at a touch to my lips and snatch my hand away from my mouth. I felt the desperation in your kiss. Fuck, it trembled through your entire body when I slid my hands around your back and dragged you up against me.

Did you think it would make me forget that you tried to cover up the fact that I scare you?

My fingers trace the outline of my lips.

God, but you taste so good, little Charlotte. You've poisoned me with that sweet mouth of yours. You'll be my undoing, but I don't give a fuck. I was obsessed before…now I'm addicted.

My phone is on the seat beside me. I'm so tempted to call you, but the time isn't right. If I fuck up now, I fuck up for good. I'll lose my chance to be with you in the way I so badly want to.

My cock hardens at the thought of being inside Charlotte. Having her pussy grip me, desperate. Hungry like her lips.

Like my soul ever since I met her. I could have devoured every inch of her supple body last night, but when I slid my hand over her tit, she pushed me away wearing a scandalized expression like she'd never considered the thought that there could be more than just kissing.

For her sake, I hope that seed is good and planted.

I reach for my phone, then snatch my hand back and twist my bottom lip with my fingers.

This street is dark. Good for me, shit for her. What the hell is she thinking walking around at night in this neighborhood? Can't she feel all those eyes on her? The predators, the criminals, the psychos?

There's so much I must show my little Charlotte. How to lie, how to control her emotions, how to overcome her phobias. I will teach her to heel, and bend, and take every inch of my cock without gagging or bleeding.

My semi becomes a raging hard-on, making me shift in my seat. I could have ignored it, forced it to go away, but then a shadow falls over the apartment window which resolves a moment later into Charlotte's silhouette.

Fuck.

She's no longer wearing her bulky clothes. In fact…I don't think she's wearing anything at all.

Temptation washes over me, too hard, too fast to push back. Groaning, I unzip my pants and haul out my dick before it snaps in two. Charlotte stands by the window, and it takes me a second staring up at her through slitted eyes before I figure out what she's doing.

Smoking something. A cigarette? No—I didn't smell tobacco smoke when I was up there yesterday. A joint?

Bad girl, Charlotte, standing there naked smoking weed. Don't you know the entire street can see you? Or don't you care?

She's on some heavy anti-depressants. Which means she probably gives zero fucks about anything right now. I could go up there, break inside, fuck her against that dirty kitchen sink of hers. I stroke my cock, imagining she's begging, screaming for me to stop…but I don't.

I climax before she's done with her joint, and by the time I've cleaned up, she's already stepped away from the window. But her light stays on.

I shouldn't stay out here all night, but I know I'll be here until dawn to make sure nothing happens to her. I need air. A quick walk up and down the street should clear out the cobwebs. I make sure not to slam the car door. Then, shoving my hands into the pockets of my trench coat to ward off the brisk wind, I head for the end of the street.

A man comes into view a few yards away. An electricity pole had blocked him from me while I was inside the car. As I draw near, I hunch my shoulders and give him a sidelong glance to make sure I don't recognize him. It pays to be careful, and tonight it pays fucking handsomely.

He notices my look and gives me an amiable nod, holding my stare.

Should have walked right past.

Should have gotten back in my fucking car and left. But this isn't a coincidence. It's a sign.

"Every Saturday night," the man says.

He looks past me, tilting his head up so he can stare into Charlotte's window. My stomach twists. Acid shoots up my throat, and for a wild second, I'm convinced I'll puke. But I breathe instead. Fight the physical response to a psychological reaction.

My Charlotte.

I look up. Her light is off. The man pushes away from the wall he'd been leaning against and gives me another smile. Like we're brothers, him and I. Sick, perverted kin lurking out here in the dark, spying on an innocent girl.

My girl.

"The fuck you say?" I growl at him.

He shrugs, laughs. Pulls a box of cigarettes from his pockets and has the fucking audacity to offer me one. "Never could resist jailbait. But that one up there, she's special."

My entire body tenses. Something is off. This isn't some homeless man hunting out free entertainment for the evening. His clothes are well cut. He has an expensive haircut. And his fingers are manicured.

The man takes back his box of cigarettes and lights himself one with a platinum Zippo. "She knows I'm down here, watching." When he speaks the smell of his freshly lit cigarette wafts to me. That and liquor, but not a drug-store make with a cheaply printed label. Something else, too, but I can't define it. "That's why she puts on a show for me every Saturday night. Stands right there in the window and flashes me her tight little body."

It's dark on this street, but even so, I should never have done what I did.

It's a culmination of so many things. The man's filthy mouth. The fact that he dared look at my Charlotte. That he called her *jailbait.*

Everything about him was *wrong.* I could smell putrid perversion coming off him in waves.

The first blow takes him by surprise, but he's ready for the second. We struggle, and I push him until his back slams into a brick wall. A pool of darkness hides us from the world as he slams his fist into my midsection, winding me. But I've fought so many like him before, and I always go for the only thing they cherish on their foul, depraved bodies.

The man lets out a pained moan when I drive my knee into his testicles, and then folds up and drops to the side like a felled tree.

Blood sings its siren call in my ears, but I can't end him. Not here, right outside Charlotte's apartment. Too many eyes, come morning. Too many questions when those eyes report the crime. So I rob the man of his possessions and stalk back to my car wearing a grimace.

His phone is a dead weight in my pocket, his wallet feather-light in comparison. I don't know why I took it, except it probably makes sense that I did. Thinking is too difficult right now—all I can smell is his blood.

Because once he was down, I didn't stop. Only the thought that I might kill him, that Charlotte might somehow find out, that she wouldn't understand I was protecting her…that stopped me.

When I climb into my car, I sit for a second and let the stink of blood suffuse the pocket of air inside the cab. Then I roll down a window and let the crisp wind chase it out.

I look up at my girl's dark window.

I'll always keep you safe, little Charlotte.

I have your file. I know what happened to you. No names, no faces, no dates—I'm not privy to that level of detail for *security* reasons, but that doesn't matter.

I know you.

I know what happened to you.

How it *changed* you.

Why you're in my class in the first place.

Soon, Charlotte Ash, you'll be back to your old self. With one important change, of course.

You'll be *mine*.

I shift in my seat, grinding my teeth. The smell of blood is so intense, it's making my mouth salivate. Which is when I realize I haven't had enough.

Not by a long shot.

6

CHARLOTTE

I wake up with a pounding heart. For a second, I think I'm still trapped in my nightmarish past. Someone holding me down, the *click-click-click* of a camera nearby. But the sound isn't coming from my memory-dream. It's coming from my living room. And when I sit up in a rush on my bed, I can see a pale glow under my bedroom door.

Someone's in my fucking house.

There's a scream bottled up in my throat, held captive by a sudden restrictive terror that refuses to let me go.

Click. Click.

No.

Please God.

It's *him*.

It's the man who locked me in his special room for seven days. The one who stole my freedom.

Not just my freedom—my life.

I choke out a sob before I can stop myself, and then clap my hands over my mouth. The light winks off. There's sudden quiet in my home. The only sound is my hitching breath.

Then footsteps.

Heavy. Hollow. Footsteps.

My hand darts out. I barely manage to control myself before sliding open my nightstand drawer.

He's getting closer.

Oh my God, he's almost here.

My hand quivers, knocking around the various knick-knacks inside my drawer as I search for the knife I've kept in there ever since I was released from the hospital.

Months it's been, and I still can't get to sleep without it. It doesn't matter where I live—I've been hopping from apartment to apartment like a fresh set of walls around me is all I need to stop replaying my week of hell.

Seven days. Almost, nearly, seven nights. But he made a mistake, and I gathered every iota of courage I possessed, and I escaped.

Malnutrition. Shock. Cut and bruised all over. Internal damage. I almost didn't make it to safety. He was on my tail for the last mile I had to run. But then there was a car, and the middle-aged couple stopped for me. I would be dead if they hadn't stopped.

Or even worse…I'd still be in that tiny, special room.

My heart shudders in my chest as I wrap my fingers around the knife's handle. I draw it out and slide my legs over the side of the bed at the same time. I try and move fluidly, like a snake, so nothing creaks or squeaks, or groans.

Hand tight around the knife.

Thump. Thump. Footsteps right up to the door.

The handle turns.

I slip under the bed in a rush as the intruder pushes open my bedroom door. I clamp one hand over my mouth, the other holding the quivering knife beside my head. Ready to jab out at his ankles if he comes close. Ready to stick it right through his fucking eye if he bends down to peek under my bed skirt.

This time, I'm ready to *kill.*

But he just stands there by the door. Not moving, not coming closer. Is he looking for me? Wondering if I'm in the closet or under the bed? Those are the only two options. I couldn't very well have climbed out of the fucking window.

I barely hold back a manic cackle.

It's as if I didn't take my medication. As if I didn't smoke that joint. I'm right back there on the edge of the world, rocking, rocking, rocking as I stare down at the black abyss of my hollow mind. It would be so easy to tip forward and just let go. Just let whatever is going to happen, happen. It'll be over soon anyway, won't it? One way or the other.

A tear flashes down my cheek and tickles its way over the back of my hand.

The intruder steps into my bedroom.

And then he closes the door behind him.

It's when he's standing less than two feet away from the bed that I smell it. Rich, metallic. It fills my bedroom like an expensive perfume.

Blood.

That scent, so strong I can taste it in the back of my throat, whips my frantic mind into a frenzy. I lash out with the knife, screaming hoarsely. The man steps back with demonic calm, the blade whisking as it brushes his pants. And then he brings his shoe down on the back of my hand, crushing my bones. My hoarse yell disintegrates into a pathetic whimper as I fight through the pain.

He wrenches the knife from my unresisting fingers, reaches under the bed, and grabs a fistful of my hair. My lungs claw for air as he hauls me out with that grip alone, but before I have enough for a new scream, he spins me around and shoves me against the wall.

Lights flash and dance in the darkness of my room.

The smell of blood lies thick in the air.

Something cold and hard touches my throat. The flat of the knife —not the edge. A warning. Just a twist of his hand and my throat is sliced.

It's too dark in here to make out anything but his shape, but I know he's big.

My frantic mind conjures up the only person I know who could logically be standing here in the middle of the night with a knife to my throat…and my bladder releases a rush of warm urine down the inside of my thighs.

Peter Monroe.

An architect, once. But something had happened in his life. Something triggered a change in him. That led Peter to start work on a top-secret project at his lake house out in the Waspwood forest. When he was done, he had a secret cavity no one knew about, that no house plans would ever show and no one—especially his victims—would ever be able to escape from.

I was victim number three.

They still haven't found the bodies of the other two girls he kidnapped, even though they searched every inch of his land for their graves.

It's him holding me against the wall. It must be. And that blood I smell in the air? Could only be the blood of another hapless victim. He's come to finish the job, to make sure I can never testify against him if some kind of miracle made that possible.

I'm convinced of all of this right up to the point where Peter dips his head and presses his lips to mine.

7

CHARLOTTE

The kiss is brief, rough. Like the intruder is claiming my mouth before he claims my body. I know it's not Peter—he never once tried to kiss me—but I don't have the bandwidth to try and figure out who the hell he is. Not now. I'm too busy struggling, too busy trying to save my life. But every elbow jab I get in, every nail scratch, every sloppy punch only seems to spur him on even more.

He doesn't care that I've pissed myself. He grips me, squeezes me right through that wet fabric. Maybe it even turns him on, because the sound he makes when he massages my pussy through my clothes is urgent and fierce.

He yanks down my pajama bottoms and shoves his knee between my legs, leaving me bare and exposed. Only then does he pause. My eyes are squeezed closed, so I don't know if he's looking down there or watching my face.

I don't want to know. He's too powerful, so there's only one way this ends, and that's all I'm praying for now.

For this to end.

His breath is warm and sweet on my face, and intensifies as he comes closer. He searches out my mouth with his again, bruising my lips with another violent kiss.

Then it hits me. I must have slipped off to sleep. I'm dreaming.

They've been happening more often these days, these darkly erotic dreams. They're never this vivid…but that's because I'm remembering them after I've woken up. But I'm *in* one right now, aren't I? Experiencing it *right* now. When you're inside a dream, it's all there is. It's your entire world. So it feels just like real life, doesn't it?

And if this is a dream, then this intruder can be anyone I want him to be.

Not my brutal captor, Peter Monroe…but someone else. Someone I actually like. Someone I wouldn't fight if they had me pushed up against a wall.

Someone like Professor Fyre.

My legs aren't trying to slam closed anymore. Instead of clamping my jaw shut, I open my lips and let Fyre in. He growls deep in the back of his throat and grabs my breasts, squeezing me through my pajamas. I whimper against his mouth, and he draws back.

He exhales a warm breath over my face, and my eyes flutter open. The way the light falls in the room, his face is in shadow, but I'd know his silhouette anywhere.

Apparently I have a superpower. I can turn nightmares into wet dreams.

Fyre shoves the first two fingers of his hand into his mouth and sucks on them. Cleaning the blood from them, I realize when he reaches down and strokes my pussy with those damp fingers.

My hand travels down his hard stomach, then I tug at the button on his jeans. I can already feel the swell of his hard cock as I try to twist open the button, and as if to tease me with it, he steps closer and crushes his erection against my stomach.

He starts finger fucking me. Filling me deeply, Fyre grinds the base of his palm against my clit. I gasp as my pussy clenches, sending tight waves of aching bliss through my core.

I lean into his thrusts, my hips rocking backward and forward. He keeps his lips on mine, fierce and demanding, as his fingers thrust harder and harder into me.

I climax before I've even had a chance to open his jeans. He pulls away from me, and I can feel his eyes on me as I come undone under his touch. His dark shadow watches as he draws out my orgasm with a skilled thumb on my clit, and watches me melt away to nothing.

Then he drags his fingers out of me and lifts a hand to his face. I can hear him sucking on his fingers again.

Before I can gather myself, before I can make sense of anything, he grabs both my thighs and wrenches them open even further. Then he ducks down and sucks my clit between his lips, biting down so hard I let out a strangled scream.

My hands are in his hair, trying to yank him away, but he simply releases that tiny nub of tender flesh and instead licks the length of my slit with a warm, hard tongue before standing.

His hand is around my throat. He pushes me back into the wall and stands there for a moment as if he's going to say something.

But he doesn't.

He squeezes my throat once, hard, and then releases me. I collapse to the floor, shaking, a confused sob dragging its way up my throat as he walks out of my apartment.

I should have woken up by now. Which means I'm not dreaming. Fyre was here. He broke into my home and—

I cut off the thought and instead lie in a puddle of piss and let myself drift away.

8

CHARLOTTE

I stare down into my cup of coffee with disgust. It's not the coffee's fault—it's the best cup I can produce in my apartment. It's *me* I'm disgusted with. It's been a week since Fyre visited me with blood on his hands. A week that I've spent alternating between hating him and hating myself. What I haven't done is go to the police.

Because for some fucked up reason, even when I think I hate him…I love him.

I thought I was getting better. I thought I was improving.

I wasn't.

I'm just as fucked up as the day I flagged down that couple's car in the woods.

Maybe even more.

At least, before, I could convince myself that my strange urges, my almost obsessive interest in sex and fucking was just a phase I was going through. I only mentioned it once in passing to my therapist, and then pretended she'd misheard me when her eyes widened. As it was, they had me under psychiatric evaluation at the hospital when I tried to slit my wrists with a scalpel I dug out of a hazardous waste bin in the ER. I wasn't going to give them any reason to keep me there indefinitely.

I'm not a psycho.

I'm *damaged.*

There's a difference.

A hard ache contracts deep in my belly. I squeeze my eyes closed, grimacing as I try to breathe through the pain. It woke me today, this pain. It's been coming steadily every few minutes. It's what I imagine contractions would be like.

Not that I'll be able to have children. Peter took many things from me…my womb was one of them.

I try a sip of coffee, but it coats my tongue like rancid oil. This is my fault. I let my new, horrifying urges take control. Instead of fighting off my attacker, I let him use me, let him bring me that brief, sickening pleasure, and then walk away scot-free.

When I woke up the next day I was still lying on the floor, the smell of urine and blood thick in the air. I barely made it to the bathroom in time to puke, and that's when I saw the smudges of blood on my face, the finger marks on my throat. After that, I could no longer convince myself it had been a dream.

My knife is gone. It makes me wonder if Fyre kept it as a memento, or so that I have less chance of defending myself the next time he visits me.

God…how many times has he actually visited me?

How many times has he been standing at the foot of my bed when I wake up groggy from the drugs, my primal instinct to survive desperate to push me out of my lethargy, but failing. How often have I woken up with crusty underwear and the vague memory of coming in my sleep?

It was him, wasn't it? He'd visit me in the middle of the night when I was too drugged up to fight him, and he'd touch me in my sleep.

I reach for my coffee again, determined to wash away the bitter taste of bile that remains. Despite the toothpaste, despite the fucking mouth wash. The cup pauses halfway to my mouth. Eyes glued to the cup, I watch in fascination as the surface of the liquid trembles like there's an earthquake on the way. I tighten my grip, but it doesn't help.

I can't live like this anymore. This isn't normal. It isn't right.

I don't know who's more fucked up—the man abusing me in the night, or the woman who *lets* him. Because I knew deep down in my heart that I wasn't dreaming. I might not have known who was in my room, who was touching me, but I knew it wasn't right.

I'll never be normal again, will I?

I slowly stand. There's sudden pressure in my head—impending tears, a migraine on the way, who knows—but it's distant. I clomp to my bathroom, my feet so heavy I can barely lift them.

Thump.

Thump.

The closer I get to my nightstand, the heavier my body becomes. It's resisting me, fighting for survival.

Like I did in Peter's little box.

I *fought*.

I fought until I couldn't anymore, and then I fought some more. But it didn't matter. He was stronger. He was faster. I didn't stand a chance.

I'll never be able to protect myself. I'll always be trying to escape.

I rip open my drawer. An orange bottle of prescription pills rolls around inside, moving so much easier now that my knife is gone. I pick it up, the drugs inside rattling as my hand shakes.

You can do this, Charlotte. Be brave. It's the only way. You want this to stop, don't you?

I'm in a new box. This one's invisible, but it's even smaller than Peter's little cavity under the basement of his lake house in Waspwood Forest. This box is so small I barely fit in.

And it's getting smaller. Closing in. Walls collapsing, trapping me.

If I don't break out, it'll smother me.

Pills rattle.

When I sleep, I'm not in the box anymore. And all I have are those lewd dreams.

It's a win-win.

9

FYRE

Charlotte hasn't been in class this whole week. It's taking all my willpower not to go to her apartment and knock on her door.

She doesn't want to see me. I crossed the line, and now she knows it too.

I don't *deserve* to see her again. I know this. I've come to terms with it. But now I'm so worried about her, I'm trying to justify breaking my own rules just to make sure she's safe.

I shift on the driver's seat, rub my fingers over my mouth. It's the middle of the day—despite my tinted windows, I shouldn't be here. Someone could spot me through the windshield, recognize me, report me. But I'm past the point of logic right now. Nothing matters but Charlotte.

I've been wracking my brain figuring out how to fix this. I can't go back in time and undo what I did, but is there a way to stop myself from getting into my car every day, every night, and driving out here, and sitting in my fucking car?

Watching her.

Protecting her.

My steering wheel creaks as I tighten my hands on the leather.

Who the fuck am I kidding? The only person she needs protecting against is *me*.

I know what my visit could have done to her, mentally. Especially someone who's been through her ordeal. But I did it anyway, because that's how fucked I am. That's how *obsessed* I am.

She will go to the police. They'll revoke my license. I'll lose my job.

And I don't give a fuck.

I still want her.

More.

Every inch.

I laugh, the sound echoing manically in the confines of my cab. Sometimes my profession is more a curse than a blessing. Curiosity got me here in the first place. I couldn't understand how a man could take the life of two people in such a violent, horrific manner and still function in society. No red flags.

Red Friday.

Those letters burn like fire across my mind, and I curl my fingers against my palms, my nails biting half-moons into my flesh in an effort to eviscerate that sudden treacherous memory.

Curiosity became a passion. It fascinated me how the human mind was so adept at concealing its own rotten depravity.

Somewhere behind me, a car alarm goes off. My eyes instantly move to Charlotte's window.

I can't take this. I have to know if she's okay. If that triggers the end of my career, of my *freedom*, I'm okay with that.

10

FYRE

"Charlotte!"

Blood sings in my ears. It drowns out all the sounds around me—my frantic panting, the shuffle of my suddenly heavy feet on the floorboards.

She tried to make it to the bathroom, but it was too far. She's laying on her back, a streak of vomit down the side of her face, more in her hair. My hands are shaking so hard I'm scared I'll hurt her as I shove her onto her side, dragging her leg up so she's in a recovery position.

I press fingers to her neck.

Breath only enters my lungs again when I feel that faint, almost indistinguishable thrum of a pulse under my fingertips, then relief washes through me in a prickle of hot and cold. I sink back on my heels and wipe my hair out of my face as I stare down at her.

In a flash, my eyes dart up to her bedroom door.

Those fucking pills.

I saw them the first night I broke into her apartment. I'm thorough. They disturbed me back then, and now I know why.

Too strong.

Too tempting.

They give her peace, but she sleeps like the fucking dead when she's taken them. Dangerous. She never even knew I came to visit her. Even when her eyes flickered open and she saw me standing by her bed, there was no recognition in her eyes.

Even when I slid my hands under the covers, she didn't—*couldn't*—resist. I didn't dare penetrate her back then—but she'd moan when I touched her tits and when I stroked her pussy through her underwear. Those sounds were the only thing that kept me going. They helped me endure the torture of seeing her in my class and not being able to touch her. Not being allowed to kiss her.

But it all became too much. When she crossed that line and kissed me the other day, the dam broke. There was no stopping the tsunami of my passion for her.

Love.

For the first time in my life, I understood.

Even now, staring down at her comatose body, her pale, puke-streaked face…I've never seen anything more beautiful.

"I love you, Charlotte," I murmur, wiping a strand of hair from her face. "I love you more than you'll ever know. And I need you in my life. Now, forever." A fond smile curls up the corners of my mouth. "You don't have to be scared anymore. I'll take care of you."

Now.

Forever.

11

CHARLOTTE

Professor Fyre looks so handsome today. He's wearing a tan blazer that brings out his olive skin and dark hair, and every time he smiles, he flashes his perfect teeth at me.

Okay, not just at me.

A pang of jealousy hits me at the thought I'm sharing Fyre's adoration with Fredericka or Graham.

But I'm a big girl.

I can handle it.

There's a lot of shit I can handle these days. Maybe my suicide attempt reset my brain or something.

That phantom pain is gone, the one where my womb used to be. That more than anything convinces me that I had a life-changing moment.

My mouth shifts to the side as Fyre beams at Fredericka's project. He crouches beside her chair just like he did with me a few weeks ago, nodding enthusiastically as she explains the deep meaning in her play-dough creation.

The dreams have stopped.

I'm wondering if they were caused by those pills I took every night. I'd lost the bottle sometime between downing half its contents and waking up freshly scrubbed in my bed a day later, but one morning they turned up on the kitchen counter.

I think I have a guardian angel.

What else could explain how clean my apartment was when I woke up from my Zoloft-induced coma? I remember getting sick multiple times—on my bed, on the floor—as I crawled toward the bathroom.

I thought it was over, then. I was in agony. Miserable. It had to be the end.

But it wasn't.

I lost consciousness and woke up to a new world. I thought it might have been Mrs. Crawford from next door. That she might have snapped out of her feline obsession long enough to notice I wasn't doing well. Maybe she was the one who found me, who cleaned me up, who tidied my house.

But that doesn't explain the fresh peonies I wake up to every morning. Someone leaves them in a vase on the kitchen table right next to a takeaway coffee and a fresh pastry. My fridge was cleaned out. Healthy ready-made meals fill the small freezer. Fresh fruit and vegetables on the shelves.

I was groggy and totally out of it that first day, and the next, and the next. But now it's like a switch has been turned on. Color suffuses what used to be a drab, gray world. And my house constantly smells like peonies.

Something bugs me, though.

My pills.

It's weird. The bottle's the same, but the pills look different. And although I do fall asleep like before, it's not the same. I wake up refreshed, and I have energy like nothing before.

Fyre straightens and glances around the class as if he's trying to spot whose project he hasn't looked at yet.

Me! Look at me!

As if he hears my desperate plea, Professor Fyre turns and looks right at me.

An arrow pierces my heart. My unrequited love for Fyre has grown so much in the last couple of weeks. I want to burst into flames every time I see him. Implode. Explode. I don't know which, but it's glorious and violent, and I can barely contain myself when he looks at me.

I squirm in my seat as he moves near, his easy smile growing an extra inch as he comes up to me.

"What do you have for me, Charlotte?"

Everything. My heart, my soul—

I clear my throat and slowly turn around the piece of paper on my desk. I expect Fyre's eyes to go to it immediately—he must be curious, right?—but instead he just keeps staring at me.

My insides pool.

How is it possible for a single look like that to make my panties wet?

"Absolute perfection," he murmurs, still with his eyes on me.

Shock turns my skin pale and cold. "Wh-what?"

Finally, ruefully, his eyes slide away from my face and settle on the paper in front of me. He stands there for the longest time, his mere presence igniting a million different nerve points through my body.

"Is it okay?" I ask, glancing between him and my drawing with mounting panic.

I should have used color. I should have tried to paint something. It's horrible. He hates it. Why did I—?

"A gift," he says.

It's insane, but at that moment, I'm convinced he's talking about the peonies that fill my home with their sweet fragrance every morning.

"You have a gift, Charlotte."

"Really?" My heart is about to explode out of my chest with pride. "It's that good?"

His hand slides onto my shoulder. I jolt at the touch, but then I lean into it, barely restraining myself from resting my head against his arm. "You certainly have talent. Come see me after class. I want to discuss something with you."

My heart climbs up my throat and lodges itself there. I'm aware I'm staring at Fyre's back as he makes his way to the front of the class, but I can't help myself.

I look down at my drawing.

It's a still life. A single peony positioned just-so on my bedroom pillow. One petal came loose and lays beside the flower. I left it there because it looked…right.

The last ten minutes of class flows by like a glacier. I'm coming out of my skin by the time the bell rings and Fyre moves to stand by the door as he greets every one of his students.

It's the last time he'll be seeing us, after all.

I take my time packing up and leave the picture for last. Lifting it, I hold it carefully and step out from behind my desk.

Across the classroom, Fyre greets the last student, steps outside into the hall, checks left and right, and then steps back inside.

My stomach flutters and then drops to my feet when he pulls the classroom door closed and locks it.

12

CHARLOTTE

Fyre stalks over to me with a grim expression on his face.

Oh my God. He's angry with me. But why? What did I do? How did I fuck this up?

The hand holding my drawing begins to tremble.

"Sir?" My voice is weak, quivering.

He doesn't answer me.

I start backing up, my legs bumping against easels and workbenches as I retreat from his looming shape.

Panic has me in its teeth, shaking me like a dog with a rat.

A second before I hit the back wall of the class, Fyre catches up to me. He rips the drawing from my fingers and slaps it down on the desk beside us.

I open my mouth to try and apologize, to explain, but there's no time.

Fyre grabs my hips and hoists me up. His body slams into mine, pinning me to the wall. I wore a dress today, and maybe that's why everything happens so fast. There's no fussing with buttons, no tugging at zips.

Professor Fyre crushes his mouth against mine hard enough to make me gasp. He rips up the hem of my dress, baring my underwear to the classroom's cool air. With a yank that leaves fabric burn on my skin, my panties are now tangled around my upper thighs.

Strong fingers graze my pussy. Fyre groans against my mouth, breaking our kiss just long enough to murmur, "You're already dripping for me."

I want to say something, but I only have one second to stare up into his dark, golden-flecked eyes before he darts forward and snatches up my lips with his. He grabs my underwear and yanks, tearing the fabric down my legs.

There's a metallic *clank* as he rips open his belt, the rasp of a zipper.

My legs wrap around his waist, and he takes it as an invitation.

Fyre parts my pussy with deft fingers before forcing the first inch of his cock inside me.

I moan, gripping his waist tighter, kissing him harder. My hands are around his shoulders, one hand fisted in his hair. I twist, desperate to hold on as he forces another inch of his thick cock into me.

I'm splitting open. Tearing apart. Pleasure and pain mingle into an indecipherable cocktail of sensation that rushes through me in a hot, aching wave.

He thrusts the last of his cock inside me, forcing my ass hard against the wall.

Filling me entirely. Possessively.

I wriggle and moan and nip at his mouth, furious at him for stopping. But I have no control over him. No control over myself.

He breaks our kiss. Moves his lips to my ear. "Why is forbidden fruit always so goddamn sweet?"

I choke instead of replying. My mind is such a mess I doubt I could form a sentence. All I manage is a pathetic, "Please."

"Please what, Charlotte?" he demands in a rough voice. "Please stop? Please fuck you harder?"

"Harder," I whimper.

He growls, and again I'm convinced he's furious at me. There's a snarl on his face when he pulls back and studies me with a condescending flick of his eyes. "You should be telling me to stop," he says. "You should be screaming for help."

I shake my head. Nip at my bottom lip. "No. I want this. I want...you."

There's a flurry of movement, then I'm on my back on the desk beside us. My dress is gathered at my waist, my underwear on the floor. Those black eyes scour me with painful intensity as Fyre grabs the straps of my dress and tugs the fabric down my breasts.

My nipples are already hard, but they constrict into little nubs at his hungry gaze. And when that dark gaze slides down, down...my pussy clenches.

His lips part, an almost-sigh whispering out of his mouth as he drags a knuckle over my pussy. "You do want me, don't you?" He lifts his hand, his eyes locked on mine as he sucks on his bent knuckle.

I start to sit up, but his hand darts out and closes around my throat as he pushes me back onto the desk. A dark, twisted reverie flashes into my mind.

A tall silhouette. Blood in the air.

I hadn't forgotten. How could I? But I'd pushed that night into the depths of my mind, to a place I never go for fear of losing my way back. So many memories buried there—when my period came on the bus, my father's death and my mother's slow demise into psychosis, my first foster family, my *last*.

Peter Monroe.

Fyre shoves two fingers deep inside me, his palm slamming against my clit.

"It was you!" It's more a confirmation than an accusation. I know it was him, but I want to know *why* it was him. What drove him to break into my house that night and do what he did. The grip around my throat is too tight for there to be much vehemence in my words, but something in my voice makes him pause.

He studies me, a smile growing on his lips. "Me," he whispers.

Then he bends over me, digs the tip of his dick into my pussy, and thrusts in balls deep.

My eyes squeeze closed as I let out a strangled yelp. There's more pain now, the ephemeral kind that burrows bone-deep inside me. I try and push him away, but he's too big, too heavy, too determined.

And when he starts fucking me, I'm too paralyzed by the

intoxicating mix of depravity and fear to keep fighting him. He peppers my jaw and lips with tiny kisses, his breath puffing over my skin with every furious thrust. My nails dig into his jacket, trying to get at his flesh, but it's too thick for me to penetrate.

My tense body melts under the force of his passion until it's only the grip around my throat keeping me in place for him. Even the pain in my belly fades, replaced with a hedonistic ache I never want to end.

"You were in my house," I say.

Fyre pauses only long enough to swipe his tongue over my chin and give me a hard kiss before he picks up his pace again. "I had to keep you safe."

"You touched me while I was sleeping."

He makes a strange sound—a laugh, a grunt, I don't know—and leans back. His hips slow until I can feel every inch of his hard cock moving in and out of my dripping pussy. "Does that sicken you?" he asks.

I open my mouth to tell him it does—that *he* sickens me—but then his thumb makes contact with my clit. My protest becomes a moan as I arch up off the desk.

"Spread those pretty legs of yours," he commands.

And for some reason, I obey.

He tears his eyes away from me, staring down where he's penetrating me. "I can't control myself around you," he says as he massages my clit hard enough to make me whimper. "You destroyed my defenses, ripped away everything that makes me human. Now there's nothing left but this..." He grimaces, grabs my hips, and rams himself into me so hard that I let out a breathless cry. "This *animal.*"

His gaze travels to my breasts, my mouth, my eyes. "But the more I try and stay away from you, the more I think about you. The more I want to do these nasty things to you."

I squirm when he touches my clit again, and let out an indignant gasp when his other hand slides down and starts stroking my backdoor. "No! Professor, please—"

"Gideon," he growls. "You will call me Gideon."

"Please...Gideon." His name feels strange on my tongue. Taboo. Erotic. *Dirty.*

And oh so fucking good.

But even though I used his name, Gideon doesn't stop. Because he isn't here anymore. It's just his spirit animal. And that beast doesn't give a fuck about my feelings or my innocence. It wants to claim every inch of me—from the sweet to the depraved.

I sob out a gasp when he forces the tip of his finger into me. My back arches a second before I wrap my legs around his waist. I hold him in place, his cock buried as deep as it can go as he begins to finger-fuck my backdoor, sending electric thrills through my entire body.

My climax is iridescent.

I yell out his name, but he slaps a hand over my mouth so nothing but a muffled moan can come out. My hips buck against him as if I can somehow wedge his cock in another inch without him splitting me open. As I unravel, I'm distantly aware of his groans, of the hand around my throat tightening, tightening.

Blackness edges my vision when my eyes eventually fly open, vignetting Gideon's carnal grimace. His eyes are on mine, locked on so hard it's as if he can see right into my soul.

His cock pumps deep inside me, filling me with his seed. There's so much it oozes out as he fucks me through his orgasm. It drips between my legs and down my crack, lubricating the finger he's still thrusting in and out of my backdoor.

"Christ, Charlotte," he growls. "You're holding me like a fucking fist."

And that's because he hasn't stopped. He's still fucking me with his dick and his finger, and it's too much. I'm coming again, and this time it's with a silent scream that clutches my body like a vise.

Gideon pulls out of me, and then something hot and wet closes over my clit.

I see stars when he sucks.

An entire galaxy opens up and swallows me whole.

"Stop, please," I whimper.

He licks me slow and hard as if he'll disobey. But then he kisses the inside of my thigh, my knee.

Gideon leans over me, finally taking his hand off my throat, and smooths back a chunk of hair from my sweat-misted face. "I love you, Charlotte Ash. Just in case there was any doubt left in your mind."

I let what he says soak in as I lay there trembling under his strong body. Then I lick my lips, shake my head.

He blinks, straightens. Waits.

I push onto my elbows and manage to come to a seat. There's a mess on the desk under my ass, and it makes the surface slippery. I grab onto him for support as I tug my straps back onto my shoulders, as I smooth my dress down my shaking legs.

With a hard swallow, I finally force the words past my throat. "What you did was wrong."

His eyes narrow, but he doesn't defend himself.

I pull my leg back, maneuvering it around him so I can slip off the table. I can barely stand, but I make my spine straight and I take my hands off him, and I stare up at him until my neck feels like it will break.

"I don't think I can ever forgive you for that."

His head tilts ever so slightly, and in just that slight gesture, I see a vast change in him. Suddenly I'm not facing my sexy therapist...I'm staring up at a darkly dangerous man.

I take a step back, my stomach bottoming out in terror, but he grabs me by the throat again. Pushes me against the wall. His lips twitch as if he's battling something, but whether it's a smile or a snarl, I can't tell.

"There is no fighting this." He leans into me. "No fighting *me*."

I open my mouth, but he doesn't give me a chance to speak.

"We were meant to be together, Charlotte. And we will be, one way or the other."

He releases me, steps back. His eyes go to the drawing on the desk. Somehow it escaped our wild fucking undamaged. He rolls it up and drops his head to smell the paper. When his eyes flicker up to me, my body responds with a host of confusing signals. My mouth dries in terror, my pussy clenches in excitement, and my heart *thuds, thuds, thuds* like a drum.

"Goodbye for now, Miss Ash."

13

FYRE

I love dismal weather, the sound of rain pattering on the roof of my sedan. Rain decreases visibility, allows people like me to blend into the shadows. I can't have anyone spot me.

Not tonight.

It's been three weeks since I said goodbye to Charlotte, and my heart hasn't stopped aching. I barely eat. Sleep is but a fond memory. My every thought, both waking and those in limbo, are of her.

The way her lips formed my name. The feel of her clamping over my cock. The taste of her arousal on my fingertips.

I haven't been to see her since that day in my classroom. I knew if I did that, I would take her whether she wanted me to or not. She already hates me. She's already terrified of me. I can't push her further away. I have to prove to her how great my love is. The lengths I will go to for her.

See, Charlotte Ash doesn't know Gideon Fyre. She only knows me as her professor. It's past time I introduced her to the real me, the man who will be at her side for eternity.

I knew what I would do the moment she strutted out of my classroom without looking back. But it's taken me three weeks to get here, to this point of no return.

I snort quietly to myself as I study the apartment building up ahead. It's not dilapidated, but it's not in the best state of repair either. I guess the rent is as reasonable here as it is back in Charlotte's apartment building.

The fact that Peter Monroe dug out his burrow this close to my Charlotte is no coincidence. Neither is the weight of his phone in my pocket.

There's nothing mysterious about the universe. There's a logical explanation for everything if you know how to connect the dots.

That night when I was outside Charlotte's apartment, the night I met the man who dared spy on her through her bedroom window— that night the stars aligned.

That was no stranger.

He was none other than the man who hurt my Charlotte. I knew it as soon as I dug up the newspaper article stating he'd been arrested in connection with a suspected kidnapping. His picture was disarming —a handsome, middle-aged man in a tasteful, if casual, outfit. The epitome of a filthy rich architect.

Emphasis on the filthy.

His case wasn't in court very long. Weeks after proceedings began, the judge declared a mistrial. A break in the chain of custody, key pieces of evidence mishandled.

Charlotte never even got to testify.

And Peter Monroe was released.

No wonder my little girl could only find peace in those white pills she swallowed every night. What sane person could ever rest knowing the monster that had stolen them, had raped and tortured them for a week, was roaming the streets?

Sometimes I wonder if I'm as much a criminal as Peter Monroe. If my sick is anything close to his sick. But then *this* will happen. I'll be holding the phone of the very man I was hunting out…and I know my purpose is so much greater than all the Peter Monroes of the world.

They're the disease. I'm the motherfucking cure.

We're not in the least alike, but we *do* have something in common. This man is *obsessed* with my Charlotte.

But not as much as I am. And I'm about to prove it.

14

FYRE

An hour goes by before Peter Monroe walks out of his apartment building. He opens an umbrella, cigarette smoke puffing out from beneath it before he climbs into his silver Mercedes Benz. White light blooms, LED's lighting up in a strip as the headlamps come on.

Then he pulls away, headed for his favorite stripper bar. It's Wednesday night, and this has been his routine for the past three weeks.

He's a loner, as so many of these perverted freaks are. Keeping to himself ensures fewer people ever become aware of just what a psychopath he is. But he craves human contact too. Lick Kitty Lick is the perfect place for him to immerse himself in humanity without drawing attention. It's a high-class bar—velvet ropes and a red carpet out front—and the *kitties* inside belong to shapely young things, prettier than most.

I park my Audi in the darkest corner of the parking lot and give Peter a few minutes to make his way inside before I follow.

His face has healed nicely since our scuffle in the street last month. The one scar that hasn't fully healed yet he keeps concealed with makeup. He was limping for a week, but after I discovered who he was I almost wish I'd killed him that night.

Almost.

If I had, he'd be dead. But there's a debt he must settle first. One he owes my darling Charlotte.

One he'll be paying before the night is up.

My lips curl up in a smile as I locate him near one of the stages, a drink in his hand and a smile on his face as he watches the girl perform for him. I slide a hand into my jacket to feel for the cool, hard length of my hunting knife. Its solidity lends me focus. Strength. Determination.

I can't wait to show Charlotte my knife. To leave its wet, cross-hatched marks over her pale skin.

I will take her to my hunting lodge. I've wanted to since the day she kissed me. But it's not the right time. It must be snowing, and from the reports I receive in my emails, the first snows haven't fallen yet.

Pushing the thought of her soft skin and those big, expressive eyes from my mind, I order a drink and keep to the shadows.

He usually stays for two hours, ending the evening with a private lap dance from whichever dancer caught his fancy. But tonight he seems agitated—he's constantly looking over his shoulder, only orders two drinks, and within an hour he's already headed for the exit.

Something spooked him. He caught wind of another predator. Of *me.* But it doesn't matter. I've locked onto him. He's already sucking on his last breath.

He's parked in a well-lit area of the parking lot, so when I come up behind him and he turns—having heard the scrape of my shoes on the tar—I'm in full sight.

Peter recognizes me instantly. His hands go up before he pushes them down at his side, his flight or fight response warring with bravado, with anger, with whatever the fuck is raging through his head.

"You!" he spits out. "I'll fucking kill you!"

I laugh.

He freezes, eyes widening, gaze searching my face. He must see something he doesn't like, because now he's backing up, reaching out blindly behind him for the handle of his car door.

I have his phone in my hand, and I press the side to make the screen turn on. I've been at this long enough to know the kind of people who can easily unlock a person's phone. I'd expected something a little more sophisticated, but Peter's pin is simply his year of birth and his favorite Red Socks player's team number.

Pathetic, just like him.

"You could try," I tell him, stepping closer. "But if anything happens to me, these pictures will end up on the FBI's desk before morning."

I keep him in my periphery as I open the phone's picture gallery and tap on one of the photos, zooming in to full screen.

Even in the yellow light of the parking lot lamp, Peter's skin goes sickly pale. But still his mouth tightens and his hands curl into fists. He's a fighter, which is why he was never convicted. People like him think they have enough money to own anything—even another human being. He doesn't think what he did to Charlotte and those other girls was wrong, just *expensive*.

My stomach turns, and bitter bile surges into my mouth.

"What do you want?" Peter snaps, his eyes in slits.

"Just a few moments of your time," I tell him, giving him a warm smile. "I have a business proposition for you."

Peter eyes me suspiciously, one side of his mouth in a sneer.

"So you wouldn't be interested in a close-knit group of friends sharing certain assets with each other? Photos, videos, *birds*." The slimy prick's eyes light up at the familiar code word. "Consider it repayment for your…injuries," I say, smiling warmly.

He nods and waves a hand for me to lead the way.

There are three types of predators in this world.

The poor who debase their bodies with alcohol and drugs which, combined with an abusive upbringing, transform those wretches into men who lurk in alleyways and pay ten-dollar hookers to suck their dirty penises.

The wealthy. People who can have everything and yet still crave what they cannot have—another's innocence. They hide right out in the open.

Then there's me.

He follows me to my car. When I grab a handful of his hair and slam it into the side of the car door as I'm opening it for him, he goes down without a sound.

15

FYRE

I'm careful. I'm intelligent. And I care so much more for Charlotte than Peter ever could. I tell him this while I'm shoving him into the little box I had prepared just for this occasion.

A gust of wind slams into the side of the barn, rattling its loose boards and sending hay dust swirling into the air.

No one's been in this barn for years. Two, possibly three. Before that, it was used for the type of activities I'm on a mission to stop. Young people chained up like dogs, treated worse than any living creature should.

I'd never keep my dog chained up. Even when I'm visiting my cabin deep in Waspwood Forest, I let Arrow roam free.

I was surprised to find out that Peter's lake house was there, but it's almost on the other side of that vast stretch of densely packed woodland. A few times this past week, I've wondered if Charlotte hadn't found the roadside, hadn't flagged down help from a passing vehicle, if she'd somehow have made it to my property.

It would have taken her a few days, but it is possible.

I wish she had. I wish she'd come straight to me and not bothered with the fucking cops.

I'd have taken care of Peter Monroe the way nature intended.

Like I'm taking care of him now.

He's long since stopped begging. I guess he smells his own death in the air like the hay and the stink of rotting wood.

"How many were there?" I ask him again.

His head lolls to the side, and it takes him a second to focus on my face. One eye is swollen shut, the other is crusted with blood. His nose sits at an angle, several deep cuts sliced into his cheeks and chin. Some of those were from my hunting knife, some from my knuckles.

I close my hand into a fist, making the tight leather glove I'm wearing creak as it stretches.

Peter's eye twitches, and his lips quickly part. "Seven."

I'm not surprised. The news report said there'd been two other girls beside Charlotte, but Peter's been doing this shit for fucking decades. The other victims would have been handled more sloppily, but I already know he committed those terrible crimes in other states, perhaps even across the border.

Only when he became this egotistical shit show on its knees in front of me, that's when he built himself a nest. A trophy case where he could keep his pretty prizes for as long as he wanted.

Or until they gave up and passed on.

His body slumps when my fist slams into his face. I lean back, huffing out a breath and forcing my eyes open wide. I need to rein myself in, but every time I think about how much this creature hurt my Charlotte, how close she was to death…

Thud.

"Okay!" Peter blubbers, a ragged sob bursting out with the word. "Twelve, all right? Twelve of them."

Christ, I'm seconds away from puking, but I force that bitterness down deep, deep as it can fucking go.

"Where are they?"

"Them? They're, they're…everywhere." Peter ducks his head, but I know he's not ashamed of what he did. On the contrary—it looks like he's hiding a smile behind the blood oozing from his freshly injured nose. I nearly hit him again, but another strike could leave him unconscious.

He's already been in those manacles for three hours. I need another four.

It's the only way I can prove myself to Charlotte.

I shrug my shoulders, crack my knuckles inside my gloves. Peter peeks up at me, and shifts a little. We both know it can't go on much longer—he's looking for a swift end, and I'm trying to drag this out as much as possible.

Not *just* for Charlotte.

This is for me too.

Catharsis. Bloodletting. Peter's pain draws the venom from my veins, renders me less harmful, less…toxic. To myself, to others.

To my dear Charlotte.

I walk away to fetch the map I left in my car. Fresh air, brisk wind, a glimpse of the stars overhead. Peter screams back in the barn. It's futile—there's no one but me to hear him.

When I come back with the map, he starts laughing. But he stops as soon as I yank off his shoes and wedge one of his toes between the jaws of a pair of pliers. I lay the map on his lap and start tracing my finger through the state we're in.

"Your first," I murmur, locking eyes with Peter as I slowly tighten the pliers against his pinkie toe. He squirms, but he's bound too tightly to pull away. "Three."

He laughs again.

"Two."

"Fuck you, you cunt!"

"One."

The crunch when I crush his toe between those steel jaws rushes through me in a swirl of adrenaline. His hoarse scream is almost as satisfying as the give when his skin bursts.

"Your first victim," I say calmly, sliding the pliers over to his other foot and gripping his pinkie toe. "Three. Two—"

"Nebraska!" he yelps. "Fuck, Omaha."

I tilt my head a little and take away the pliers, grabbing a worn notebook out of my trench coat and flipping it to a new page. "Be precise," I tell him as I note down the place.

Peter tells me everything. I want to stop him—fuck knows I don't want to know what the hell he did to little Yolly before he tossed her in a shallow grave in Gifford Point, but it makes him feel better, and at least I'll be able to give her family some closure.

I move away from his chair and make a call, relaying all the information he just gave me—sparing the gory bits, of course—and then head back.

"Good. You're doing well, Peter." I let out a soft sigh and stare down at his mangled toe. "Pity you had to lose an appendage over this. I hope you've learned your lesson."

He nods, chokes a little. "Please, just let me—"

"Victim number two."

Clearing his throat, Peter glances up at me for a second as if he's considering.

I crouch down in front of him, tapping his knee with my cell phone. "Let me be straight with you, Mister Monroe. I'm part of a nationwide task force assigned to find people like you—" tap "—and obtain pertinent details. Want to know who I just called?" I lift my phone.

Peter's eyes are shadowed. He says nothing, does nothing. Just stares pure hate at me like a blowtorch.

"The FBI, Mister Monroe. They have agents on the ground in every state. They're on the way to Gifford Point as we speak. Within the hour, they'll have found Yolly. Or…"

Tap. Tap. Tap.

"Or I'll know you lied to me." I stab out with the pliers, burrowing the blunt point into his shin.

Peter flinches, but his body is already coursing with endorphins—his senses are dulled to the pain.

For now. But in about twenty minutes, he'll be fresh as a fucking daisy.

He grimaces at me, shakes his head. "What's the fucking point? You're gonna kill me anyway. Might as well do it now." He hacks up a mouthful of spit and aims it for my face, but I'm already standing. It hits my pants, just to the right of my crotch.

Nausea wells in me at the thought of his contaminated spittle being in contact with me, even through my thick jeans. But I ignore the damp spot.

"I wish I could kill you," I say quietly, boring into his eyes with a frustrated gaze. "But that's a line I can't cross. Not if I want to keep doing what I'm doing. And I'm sure you know by now, Mister Monroe, I *really* enjoy what I do."

There's just enough truth in the statement that I come across as genuine. Plus, my frustration is real. If I don't play this right, those families will never know what happened to their loved ones.

"So are we doing this?" I hold up the bloody pliers.

Peter's jaw tics, then he looks down.

"She's not in Omaha," he mutters.

Something hot and thick floods through me.

It's relief, and just a little bit of hope.

I take out my phone, make as if I'm typing out a message. "Still in Nebraska?" I ask.

"Yeah," Peter says through a rueful huff. "You know Geneva?"

"I don't," I say, not even looking up. "But I'm sure they do."

16

FYRE

A bitter wind chases me into my house while my chocolate Lab, Arrow, howls and tries to lick me to death. The instant I snap my fingers, though, she falls into a sit, her tail sweeping the hardwood floors with subdued enthusiasm.

"Good to see you too, beautiful," I murmur, as I unwrap my dark scarf from around my throat and hang it up on the coat stand. My trench coat goes over it, and I make a mental note to get it to the dry cleaners tomorrow.

It's black, so blood doesn't show, but I'd prefer not to think about how much of Peter Monroe's blood I'm walking around with.

I pat my thigh through my jeans as I start down the hallway, and Arrow darts after me like her namesake, her toenails click-clacking on the wood.

"Did you eat already?" I enter my kitchen and head straight for the kettle. It's two in the morning, but I'm too wired to go to bed. I'll most likely not sleep at all tonight—no point in trying.

But I'm frozen to the bone, grimy, and could use a hot toddy and a shower.

Arrow nuzzles my hand until I take her box of treats off the shelf and feed her a biscuit. She slobbers over my hand—no amount of training can reduce the amount of saliva a dog produces, I've found—and stares up at me with her big, beautiful eyes.

"I'm freezing," I tell her. "We're not going for a walk. You'll have to wait until the morning."

She sits and lifts a paw, panting quietly.

"Christ," I mutter, shrugging my shoulders inside my sweater. "You'll be the death of me yet, you mutt."

Arrow dashes straight to the kitchen door, staring up at where her leash hangs from a hook on the wall.

She's too intelligent by half, but I wouldn't want it any other way. I've had her since she was a pup.

I'll never forget the day I found her. Sometimes I look at her and all I can see is a dirty, bedraggled dog limping toward me out of the dark.

I thump my fist into the wood beside the door, and Arrow shifts her eyes from the leash to me, her tail slowing a little. She barks once, loud, as if to scold me for having bad thoughts.

Ruffling her ears, I slot the leash into her collar and lead her out of the kitchen door and down the cobbled path heading to the front gate.

When we get back from our walk I'm even colder than before. The wind hasn't let up one bit, and I can taste the promise of snow in the air.

I let Arrow back inside our home and go to turn on the kettle again. Arrow's nails click on the floor as she heads straight for our bedroom.

She's getting on in years, so I'm not in the least surprised when she's already snoring on the bottom of my queen-sized bed.

I shake my head and turn on the shower.

As I'm stepping out, a gust of wind hits the bathroom window. And, with it, a burst of sludgy snow.

I stare at it for a moment, and then my lips curl up in a smile.

"Guess what, Arrow?" I say as I walk back into the room, rubbing a towel through my hair. She stops snoring, but doesn't look in my direction. She doesn't know if the news is important enough for me to disturb the comfortable-as-fuck position she found.

"We're going hunting."

Arrow's head whips up, her eyes wide, her jaw parted as she lets out a huff.

"And this time it won't just be the two of us."

My lab lets out a soft bark, and then her head flops down again.

"You'll love her," I murmur as I take a sip from my steaming cup. "Trust me."

17

CHARLOTTE

The rain dilutes my tears until I barely taste them. I should have my hood up, but the sting of the cold drops is the only thing stopping me from returning to my apartment and ending my life. The first few days, I didn't miss the peonies. Not one bit. But before the end of the week, their absence became a black void in my mind.

If I'd had friends, I would have turned to them for comfort. Had my parents not died a few years ago, I'd have called them.

But I have no one. Charlotte Ash is alone in this world, and as the days dragged on, that black void consumed the tattered shreds of my soul until there was nothing left but a hollow vessel, waiting to be filled.

I've tried everything, but nothing fills it.

I shouldn't be out this late at night, but I'm hoping the diner is still open. I'm hoping I can take a seat, order something, and it will fill me. Even though I can't taste anything anymore, hunger still gnaws at me.

I can't seem to fill that either.

I grimace as tight pain constricts inside my womb. That came back too, a few days ago. I know it's psychological now, but that's *all* I know. I have no idea how to stop it, what caused it, or if I'll ever be free of it.

It's my punishment for enjoying what Fyre did to me. For letting him put his hands on me and not fighting him off tooth and nail.

The street is empty. I'm the only one who's dared to come out on such a shitty night.

At least, that's what I think until I hear the splash of footsteps behind me.

My heart strangles me as it leaps into my throat. When I speed up, my pursuer effortlessly keeps pace. I don't dare look back in case the sight of my stalker makes me freeze up. Instead, I scan the street ahead for help.

But there's no one in sight. No buildings to dart into. Just solid brick walls left and right. One stationary car a few yards up the road—unoccupied. I can't run. Not yet. I'll just start a chase. The element of surprise is all I have. If I could slip out of sight and then sprint away...?

When I see an alley mouth gaping black ahead, I take it.

The *splash-thud* of my footsteps is too loud in my ears. That and my own frantic breathing is all I can hear.

I've lost them. I must have. Relief washes over me—even icier than the rain hurtling down into the narrow alley. But it vanishes an instant later when I realize the darkness ahead isn't an empty void like my soul. There's substance to it.

I barely get my hands out in time. I crash into a wall, the bricks scraping over my palms, slicing deep. I spin around, already knowing what I'll see.

A silhouette stands in the mouth of the blind alley. It watches me for long, rain-pounding seconds, and then moves closer. Not hurrying. Just walking.

The closer it gets, the tighter my chest becomes. The more my fingers dig into the bricks behind me, as if testing their solidity.

And then I recognize him.

Professor Fyre.

My relief is nothing but a brief, warm wave. Because the closer he gets, the more real he becomes. Memories of him fill my mind, mocking me for feeling hope. I'm trembling by the time he stops in front of me.

"Wh-what are you doing here?"

I wish my voice didn't quaver.

I also wish I hadn't left my apartment tonight.

"I have a gift for you," he says.

I try to scowl at him, but he doesn't seem to notice. Fyre reaches into his pocket. My heart climbs up my throat, followed by a rush of warm, acidic bile.

This is it. It's finally over.

I squeeze my eyes closed so I can't see the knife or the gun or whatever it is he's going to kill me with. Light bathes my eyelids. I struggle to keep them closed, but finally, they pop open, ready to confront my attacker.

I'm staring at a cell phone. There's an image on the screen. For a second, I have no idea what I'm looking at.

And then the bile that was sitting in the back of my throat, kept in place by my pounding heart, gushes into my mouth. I turn my head, puking violently onto the filthy ground beside me.

"He'll never touch you again, Charlotte. He'll never touch *anyone* ever again."

My stomach contracts, but there's nothing left. I haven't eaten in days. All that was in there was that one mouthful of stomach acid. I push myself up using the bricks as support and lean my head back against their rough surface.

"And now it's my turn?" I whisper.

Fyre cocks his head as a strange smile plays on his lips. "You don't recognize him," he muses quietly. "It's understandable. Death changes everything." He looks at the phone, then juggles it in his hand. When he turns it to face me, I instantly look away, squeezing my eyes shut with a terrified whimper. "Look at him, Charlotte. Who do you see?"

Fyre needs to be humored. Perhaps, if I do what he says, he'll let me go. So I look. And I do my best to forget that the image I'm looking at is a severed head. Fyre helps—his finger is obscuring the bottom of the photo. I'm left with a view of a man's face from the chin up.

Slack. Distended. Mouth gaping. Eyes open—empty and sad.

I blink, and suddenly it's not just a head. Not just a dead person. I recognize his nose. The shape of his eyes. A gasp rattles in my throat. I wrench the phone from Fyre's hand and stare at it with bug eyes.

Peter Monroe.

"How…"

Gentle fingers take the phone out of my hand. Fyre grabs my chin and tips my head up. Then he strokes the side of my face, his knuckles drawing warm tingles over my skin.

"He suffered for his sins, my girl." Fyre puts his mouth by my ear. "Not nearly as long as he made you suffer, but my time with him was limited." He kisses my neck, his voice somehow managing to reach me over the roar of blood in my ears.

"Seven hours for seven days." Another kiss, this one softer than the last.

How did he know about Peter Monroe? How did he *find* him? Why would he—

"I did it for you." Fyre draws back, cups my face in his hands. "All of this, I did for you."

We stare at each other as the rain drums down around us. I feel weightless and so heavy at the same time. Clear-headed, but foggy. I have no words for what Fyre did for me. It's criminal. Psychotic. And so fucking heroic, I can't breathe.

I dart forward, grabbing him up in a fierce hug. "Thank you," I mumble against his damp jacket. He slides his arms around my shoulders, hugging me back just as hard.

"My pleasure," he says, stroking my head.

I know I should stop touching him, but it's impossible to let him go. Where my head is, I can hear his heart beating.

Thud.

Thud.

Thud.

And I know, somehow, that it beats for me.

Me…and *only* me.

But this man is a killer. A psycho. My *stalker*. I should be running from him, not hugging him. Something approaching logic slithers back into my mind, and I bring up my hands, pushing against his chest.

It doesn't matter what his intentions were, or how much gratitude I feel for what he did. Murdering Peter Monroe was a crime. Two wrongs don't make a right.

But when I push, nothing happens. Fyre is holding me too tight.

When I begin to struggle, he lets out a patient, "Shh," and strokes the top of my head. Then he puts his hand in his pocket.

I open my mouth to scream, and that's when he presses a handkerchief over it. Immediately, an acrid stench hits my nose. My lips and tongue go numb, and it feels as if every ounce of blood leaves my face at once. A harsh tingle runs through my head, down my arms, through my entire body.

My spine melts, and suddenly I'm limp in Professor Fyre's arms. The darkness we are nestled in in this blind alley starts converging in on me, pressing tighter and tighter, suffocating me.

I'm dying, but it's gentle. Calm, almost.

The sky wheels above my head as Fyre lifts me, and I feel nothing when he cradles me against his chest. My eyes slide closed a moment before I hear him whisper, "I love you, Charlotte Ash. And with time, you'll learn to love me too."

The End

Charlotte & Fyre's story continues in Under Fyre, available now at your favorite retailer.

MORE BY LOGAN FOX

For more books by this author, reading order, playlists, trigger warnings, socials, and more…please visit:

https://authorloganfox.com